SELECTED ENSEMBLE SONATAS

Recent Researches in the Music of the Baroque Era is one of four quarterly series (Middle Ages and Early Renaissance; Renaissance; Baroque Era; Classical Era) which make public the early music that is being brought to light in the course of current musicological research.

Each volume is devoted to works by a single composer or in a single genre of composition, chosen because of their potential interest to scholars and performers, and prepared for publication according to the standards that govern the making of all reliable historical editions.

Subscribers to this series, as well as patrons of subscribing institutions, are invited to apply for information about the "Copyright-Sharing Policy" of A-R Editions, Inc., under which the contents of this volume may be reproduced free of charge for performance use.

Correspondence should be addressed:

A-R Editions, Inc.
315 West Gorham Street
Madison, Wisconsin 53703

RECENT RESEARCHES IN THE MUSIC OF THE BAROQUE ERA · VOLUME XXIII

Dario Castello

SELECTED ENSEMBLE SONATAS

Part I

Edited by Eleanor Selfridge-Field

A-R EDITIONS, INC. · MADISON

Copyright © 1977, A-R Editions, Inc.

ISSN 0484-0828 *(Recent Researches in the Music of the Baroque Era)*

ISBN 0-89579-090-4 (Set, Parts I and II—Volumes XXIII and XXIV)
ISBN 0-89579-091-2 (Part I—Volume XXIII)

Library of Congress Cataloging in Publication Data:

Castello, Dario, fl. 1621-1644.
   [Sonate concertate in stilo moderno. Selections]
   Selected ensemble sonatas.

   (Recent researches in the music of the baroque era ;
v. 23-24 ISSN 0484-0828)
   Includes bibliographical references.
   CONTENTS: pt. 1. Sonatas from Sonate concertate,
book I (1621): Sonata 3 for two treble instruments.
Sonata 5 for treble instrument and trombone. Sonata 9
for two violins and bassoon. Sonata 12 for two violins
and trombone. [etc.]
   1. Chamber music. 2. Trio-sonatas. I. Series.
Recent researches in the music of the baroque era ;
v. 23-24.
M2.R238   vol. 23-24   [M178]   77-11128
ISBN 0-89579-090-4 (set)

Contents

Preface

Very little information exists concerning the life of the Venetian composer Dario Castello. Extant title pages to his works provide the only firm evidence of his existence. They indicate that he was the leader of a group of wind instrumentalists (*piffari*) which may or may not have been associated with San Marco. Title pages also show that he had become a musician at San Marco by 1627, acquired the title "Don" between 1625 and 1627, and continued to lead a *piffaro* group in 1627. Castello evidently carried on these activities with little change until he died or retired between 1656 and 1658.

It seems strange that there is so little concrete evidence of the life of a composer whose works were as often published and reprinted as Castello's. Other musicians with the surname Castello flourished at the same time as Dario did. Giovanni Battista Castello, an instrumentalist, seems to have had a career that paralleled what is known of Dario's career as a composer. For a detailed discussion of the problem of the Castello biography, the reader is referred to the present editor's "Dario Castello: A Non-Existent Biography."[1]

The Music

Except for a solo motet in the Simonetti anthology *Ghirlanda sacra* (1625), Castello's works are all instrumental ones. They first appeared in two volumes with the title *Sonate concertate* (Books I and II). The record of seventeenth-century reprints of these volumes is impressive. Using the sigla employed in Claudio Sartori's *Bibliografia della musica strumentale italiana*,[2] all known editions of Castello's sonatas with their present locations and conditions are listed as follows:

1621n *Sonate concertate in stilo moderno à 2 & 3 voci, libro primo.* Venice, 1621. No surviving copy.

1629e Book I (reprint). Venice, 1629. Complete[3] in the Biblioteka Uniwersytecka, Wrocław.

1629f *Sonate concertate in stil moderno per sonar nel organo ouero clauicembalo con diuersi instrumenti. A 1. 2. 3. & 4. voci, libro secondo.* Venice, 1629 (the dedication to the Hapsburg Ferdinand II is dated September 1627). Lacking the basso continuo only[4] in the Biblioteka Uniwersytecka, Wrocław.

1644e Book II (reprint). Venice, 1644. Complete in the Bodleian Library, Oxford; damaged copy in the Biblioteca Nazionale Centrale, Florence.

1656e Book II (reprint). Antwerp, 1656. Quarta Parte only in the British Library, London.

1658a Book I (reprint). Venice, 1658. Complete in the Bodleian Library, Oxford.

1658b Book I (reprint). Antwerp, 1658. Complete in the Library of the Dean and Chapter, Durham Cathedral.

Sonatas 3 and 4 of Book II also exist, with a bass part derived from the basso continuo, in MS EM (= Estensischen Musikalien) 83 in the Austrian National Library, Vienna. This source also contains instrumental pieces by Carlo Fedeli (ca. 1622-85), Giovanni Legrenzi (1626-90), and Johann Rosenmüller (1620-84). The era during which all three of these composers were simultaneously active in Venice would have been ca. 1672-82.

The following sonatas by Castello are already available in modern editions: (1) Sonata 4 of Book I, "Quarta sonata à due," ed. Franklin Zimmerman (Dartmouth Collegium Musicum, Series 4), Hanover, N.H., 1966; and (2) Sonatas 1 and 2 of Book II, "Due sonate á soprano solo," ed. Friedrich Cerha (Diletto Musicale, No. 37), Vienna, 1965.

Sonatas 3, 5, 9, and 12 of Book I appear in Part I of the present edition, and Part II contains Sonatas 7, 11, 12, 15, 16, and 17 of Book II.

Castello's Style and Its Origins

The decade between 1620 and 1630 was one of the most productive periods in Venetian musical history. The musical atmosphere surrounding Castello was dominated by the Mantuan composer Claudio Monteverdi (1567-1643), who served as *maestro di cappella* at San Marco for the last thirty years of his life. His consuming interest was in vocal music—opera, the accompanied madrigal, and the motet. Monodic writing was so popular at this time that the solo motet and a new genre called the cantata offered the parish church and private chamber the semblance of opera without demanding the same grand proportions and lavish resources. Monodic writing was also applied in instrumental music, but only after it had been used in vocal music.

As a vocal composer, Monteverdi's influence on Venetian instrumental music is pervasive but indirect; no exclusively instrumental works by him are known. His use of diverse combinations of instruments in his first opera, *Orfeo* (Mantua, 1607), is well known, but the roster of instruments in his operas written for Venice is much more modest. His theories on music, ostensibly founded on the teaching of Plato, emphasize the importance of the text, which of course is absent in instrumental music. Nonetheless, Monteverdi's efforts to recreate three emotional states or affects—the agitated (*stile concitato*), the peaceful (*stile molle*), and the evenly tempered (*stile temperato*)—provided several cues for instrumental composers. The use of rapid repetitions of a single chord to suggest the warlike *stile concitato* found a permanent place in the Italian instrumental repertory of the seventeenth century. During his Venetian years Monteverdi and his circle also cultivated the accompanied duet, the instrumental equivalent of which was the trio sonata.

In addition to the stylistic examples offered by vocal composers of his time, Castello inherited two conflicting instrumental traditions from earlier Venetians. One was the canzona repertory associated in particular with Giovanni Gabrieli (ca. 1557-1612). The other was the improvisatory tradition cultivated by ensemble instrumentalists in the sixteenth century. In Venice the canzona literature was produced chiefly by organists, who were relatively strict in applying the precepts of music theory. By contrast, ensemble instrumentalists, relegated to the lowest niche of the musical hierarchy and trained by example, were very adventurous; their bent was more toward the sonata, with its greater possibilities for display.

The hallmark of the Gabrielian ensemble canzona was its emphasis on contrast. Contrast, the dominating principle of Venetian culture in the later sixteenth and early seventeenth centuries, was central to the *chiaroscuro* paintings of Tintoretto and his followers and to the antiphony of the polychoral Mass and motet. The bulk of canzonas from Gabrieli's generation are of two types—those in which contrast is achieved through opposition of tutti and solo and those in which contrast is achieved by alternations in texture (polyphonic or homophonic), meter, tempo, and dynamics. Contrasts of the first type predominate in Castello's sonatas, but alternating tempos and dynamics are also plentiful.

The virtuoso tradition of the sixteenth century emphasized improvisation. The preferred formulas of improvisation and general advice on particular instruments were given in such works as Silvestro di Ganassi's *La Fontegara* (1535) for recorder and his two-volume manual on the viol (1542-3). Other works include Girolamo Dalla Casa's *Il vero modo di diminuir* (2 vols., 1584-5), and Giovanni Bassano's *Ricercate, passaggi, et cadentie* (1585/6) and *Motetti, madrigali et canzoni francese . . . diminuiti per sonar* (1591/2). Dalla Casa and Bassano were both cornettists. Dalla Casa organized the first orchestra at San Marco in 1567/8 and directed it until his death in 1601. He was succeeded by Bassano, who served until his death in 1617. Both were almost certainly the masters of wind bands as well.

While solo virtuosity in Castello's works was no doubt encouraged by the examples of vocal monody all around him, much of the specific content of virtuoso passagework seems to have derived from the division techniques of the sixteenth century. Castello's notated ornamental lines were probably often produced by improvisation in the performance of ostensibly simpler pieces, and Castello's sonatas give valuable indications of instrumental techniques and players' capabilities. Yet as they stand, the sonatas must have been somewhat more difficult than what most instrumentalists of the time were accustomed to playing. In the 1629 reprint of Book I, Castello added a sarcastic note recommending that the music be practiced prior to its performance and assuring his readers that practice would not rob the works of their soul.

The virtuoso passagework in Castello's sonatas is different, though no less technically demanding, than that in many other works of the era. First, he emphasizes wind instruments—the cornett, trombone, and bassoon—in addition to usually unnamed instruments of treble range. Second, he sometimes focuses on a duet (in keeping with the fashionable vocal duet), rather than on a solo, for virtuoso display. Third, except in the case of the two solo sonatas, Nos. 1 and 2 of Book II, Castello's virtuoso parts are always silhouetted against the background of an ensemble in which all the members are soloists by turns. Thus an equality of importance is maintained between parts and the resultant character of Castello's ensemble sonatas is altogether different from that of solo sonatas of the same era.

An occasional feature of Castello's style is the gentle grouping of movements by the use of thematically similar incipits. The Affetto, p. 4, [Allegro], p. 4, [Moderato], p. 5, and Adagio, p. 9, of Sonata 3, Book I and the Allegro, p. 28, Adagio, p. 33, and Allegro, p. 34, of Sonata 12 of Book II illustrate this kind of grouping. It seems unlikely that the dance suite was responsible for this trait, since Castello does not preserve the theme throughout a movement and since dance music was little encouraged in Venice at this time; exceptions, such as those from Marini's repertory, are often traceable to the patronage of German royalty or Italian academicians.

The Works in This Edition

The works in this edition illustrate the full range of Castello's styles. In general the pieces for three or four instruments are superior in workmanship and more elaborate than those for one or two, and those of Book II are more interesting than those of Book I. Taken as a group, Castello's sonatas indicate what kind of instrumental ensemble music was popular on the Continent between 1620 and 1660. The only Italian contemporary with a comparable record of reprints was Girolamo Frescobaldi (1583-1643), much of whose repertory was for keyboard. Furthermore, Castello's works testify to the ability of performers, especially wind instrumentalists, in Venice at the time of Monteverdi and during the formative years of Venetian opera; there are curiously few wind parts in surviving Venetian operas from before 1670. The sonatas also help to establish the lines of continuity in the Venetian instrumental tradition from Gabrieli to Vivaldi in a way that no other works of the same era seem to do.[5] With these works, the concerted sonata emerges as an alternative to the solo sonata.

The individual works in this edition are discussed below.

The Sonatas of Book I

Sonata 3 illustrates Castello's earliest style. No instrumentation is specified. In the opening section the *Canto secondo* repeats the *Canto primo* exactly; even their solo sections are identical. The imitative procedures are simple, although since fugal restatements were unusual at this time the stretto in the opening movement is worthy of note. The concluding section of echoes is a trait taken directly from the ensemble canzona. Because of a rough similarity of opening themes, this work can be compared with Sonata 17 of Book II.

Sonata 5 begins to show some independence of parts. For example, the solos of the *Canto primo* and the trombone, while similar, are in different keys. Canons at the twelfth are conspicuous. The contrast of fast polyphonic sections with slow homophonic ones is another feature that derives from the ensemble canzona.

Sonata 9 is one of the most impressive works in Book I and the work with the most ambitious bassoon part in Castello's repertory. The bassoon solo is especially noteworthy. The bassoon (*fagotto*) was a popular instrument in Venice throughout the baroque era. The earliest specific scoring for it occurs in a posthumously published vocal work by Gabrieli ("Jubilate Deo," 1615). Castello, Marini, Gabriel Usper (fl. 1609-23), and Giovanni Picchi (ca. 1572-1643) all included parts for the bassoon in works for instrumental ensembles that were published between 1618 and 1625. The *pp* (originally *pianin*) markings in the last movement of Sonata 9 are unusual for the time, although this dynamic gradation was used more than a century earlier in a lute book (ca. 1517) of the Brescian nobleman Vincenzo Capirola.[6]

Thematic contrast betwen violins and trombone, an absence of solo parts, and the *da capo* structure of Sonata 12 suggest that it was modeled on a sub-species of ensemble canzona used by Gabrieli and others. The work was dedicated to the priest Giacomo Finetti (d. 1631), who was *maestro di cappella* at the church of the Frari in Venice from ca. 1613 until his death. The conjunction of parallel thirds and a simple bass part in the Adagio (p. 46) and in the closing Presto (p. 62) may have been intended as imitations of the *lira da braccio* (a bowed instrument with two drone strings) and bagpipe, respectively. Both instruments had symbolic importance in madrigal poetry, and imitations of them occurred in a sonata for two violins and bassoon by Gabriel Usper (1619). Passages similar to these also occur in the posthumous Canzona No. 11 *à 8* (1615) by Gabrieli.

The Sonatas of Book II

Sonata 7 is a *da capo* work for unnamed treble and bassoon that shows Castello's progress with the two-voice medium. Most of the work's motives derive from the opening subject; this kind of derivation is characteristic of many other works in Book II.

In Sonata 11, contrast is achieved through alternations in tempo, instrumentation, and theme, rather than through the opposition of tutti and solo. A sequential motive runs through various parts of the work. Note might be made of the "Molto adagio" (originally "Adagio adagio") passage at the end.

Scored like Sonata 11 for two violins and trombone, Sonata 12 shows further possibilities of that instrumental combination. The sextuplet divisions in the solos follow patterns probably in use for a century but rarely seen in printed music. The use of a ritornello after each virtuoso passage is unusual for Castello, although the practice was well known in vocal music. Here it is a unifying feature of secondary importance, since there is also a condensed recapitulation of the opening fugue.

Sonatas 15 and 16 were almost certainly intended as a pair; although they are contrasting in style, they are both written for an ensemble of four "bowed" instruments. Sonata 15 is solemn in character and stresses imitative counterpoint. A hymn-like Adagio introduces a series of four fugues, each initiated by a different member of the ensemble. The four subjects are interrelated, and divisions on similar episodic material over a pedal point lead each fugue to a deceptive cadence.

In contrast to Sonata 15, Sonata 16 emphasizes homophony and non-imitative counterpoint. At times, instruments are used in pairs, providing a natural context for the double-subject fugato that precedes the recapitulation. The homophonic writing of the duple meter movement is of the *stile concitato* variety and can be compared with passages from Monteverdi's *Combattimento di Tancredi e Clorinda* (1624). A few of the melodic figures in the treble voice resemble the bird calls cultivated in instrumental music of the eighteenth century.

Sonata 17 is the most impressive representative of the echo sonata (or canzona) species among Castello's works, and it is probably the piece of music for which Castello was best known. It was placed first, preceding Sonata 1, in both reprints of Book II. The full ensemble is heard only in the final movement, and the echoing instruments, which were no doubt supposed to be offstage, do not play in the first, second, and fourth movements. In the first movement the three motives that form the opening entry are developed individually. This thematic technique had been used since the middle of the century to link movements within sonatas; it was also used to regulate the tutti-solo relationship in some early concertos of the Venetian repertory.

Castello's influence was strong both in and outside of Venice. In Venice Massimiliano Neri (1615?-66) and Carlo Fedeli (ca. 1622-85) were especially indebted to Castello's techniques. Castello's procedures and scoring are also visible in the posthumous ensemble sonatas (1641) of Giovanni Battista Fontana (ca. 1592-1631), a Brescian with connections in Padua. Serial solos in sonatas for a mixed wind and string ensemble were characteristic of the German composers Philipp Friedrich Buchner (1614-69) and Matthias Weckmann (1621-74). The inclusion of works by Castello in MS EM 83, which must date from the 1670s or later, gives some indication of how long Castello's reputation survived him. Certainly Castello's emphasis on virtuoso scoring for winds was a milestone on the way to the oboe and bassoon concertos of Vivaldi, Albinoni, and Alessandro Marcello, and Castello's concept of the concerted sonata seems to have contained the seed of the chamber concertos of eighteenth-century Venice.

Performance Practice

Instrumentation

Until the second decade of the seventeenth century published works for instrumental ensemble were usually intended for instruments of homogeneous timbres. The brass ensemble had been more popular than the string ensemble in Venice, and the bassoon seems to have been the only really popular woodwind instrument. One of Castello's chief interests was in combining instruments of different timbres; this should be remembered by performers making substitutions in instrumentation.

The modern equivalents of the instruments for which Castello scored are violin, viola, tenor violin, cello, cornett, tenor and bass trombone, and bassoon. Castello did no specific scoring for recorders; his works were probably intended for performance in church services. Giovanni Battista Riccio (fl. 1609-21) and Picchi are the only Venetian composers who wrote for recorder in this era. Recorders were used in wind bands, private chambers, and at state banquets.

Castello rarely scores below c' for violin, although exceptions do exist in Sonatas 15 and 16 of Book II. Castello's highest pitch for violin is c'''. Castello's *violetta* seems variously to have been an alto violin (whose modern equivalent is the viola) or a tenor violin.[7] The *violetta* part is scored in various clefs, and on some occasions it descends far below the compass of the alto violin. Such a part would suit the obsolete tenor violin which was commonly tuned an octave below the ordinary violin. In the absence of a tenor violin, a cello should be used. Although the Italian term *viola* has sometimes been thought to represent the tenor violin, this evidently was not the case for Castello or other Venetians of the time. In Castello's music, the lowest string of the *viola* is rarely used; in some cases, however (e.g., Sonata 7 of Book II), its part descends to C. Castello's *viola* seems to be an early species of the cello.

Special problems of terminology occur in Sonatas 15 and 16 of Book II, which are both scored for *violino*, two *violette*, and *viola*. Idiom and terminology both suggest that these works were for members of the violin family, but Castello gives the generic indication *"per strumenti d'arco"* ("for bowed instruments"), which certainly does not exclude the use of viols. Viols were little used in Venice at this time, although it was not unknown for violins to be used in treble parts in combination with viols in bass parts.[8] Moreover, Castello's Book II was dedicated to the Emperor Ferdinand II of Austria, whose orchestra included both violins and viols. Thus Castello, who was unusually careful in his use of terminology, must have wanted to be non-restrictive here.

Castello seems to have scored for only two of the several sizes of trombones that were used in Venice through the 1620s.[9] His parts for trombone appear in either tenor or sub-bass clef, and the *tessitura* is usually G-g'. The trombones in use in the seventeenth century were significantly more mellow than the modern variety. Mutes may be desirable in performance to give the proper dynamic balance.

Oboes may be used in place of cornetts, but not with historical impunity, since they were not in use in Venice until about 1690. Shawms, like recorders, were used in secular performances in Castello's time but rarely in connection with worship.

While the popularity of the trombone and cornett was receding in the 1620s, that of the bassoon was increasing. Accordingly, Castello scored for this two-keyed instrument with considerable relish. Its *tessitura* is C-g'.

The basso continuo realizations provided here are relatively simple; they can be enhanced by the performer or superseded altogether. Although Castello's basso continuo is provided for either harpsichord or organ, its idiom is much better suited to the latter. It may be that Castello mentioned the harpsichord merely as an acknowledgment of its emergence in the seventeenth century. If the basso continuo realizations are played on an organ, the registration should be kept simple. Works such as these would usually have been accompanied on a chamber organ. Venetian organs of Castello's time were modest instruments with a few 4' and 8' stops, a flute stop, and no independent pedals. To what extent the keyboard continuo was reinforced by ensemble instruments in Castello's time is unknown. There is so much duplication between bass and basso continuo parts in many works that no ensemble reinforcement may seem necessary. However, reinforcement is especially desirable when the keyboard accompaniment is by harpsichord. If a harpsichord is used, tied chords and notes should be treated as untied. The cues in Sonata 12 of Book I and Sonata 17 of Book II seem to imply the general presence of a reinforcing instrument. In addition to double bass and gamba, trombone, bassoon, and archlute were used as accompaniment instruments in Venice.

That many Castello sonatas are temperamental in character is demonstrated by the unusually liberal use of tempo and dynamics indications in the music. Dynamics indications were known in the sixteenth century, but tempo indications were little used before 1615. In the Renaissance, tempo and meter were indistinguishable, since all meters were related to the human pulse (= ♩) and thus interrelated to one another. In a meter signature the upper figure indicated how many breves in a new section were equivalent to the number of old breves expressed in the lower figure. Thus, 3/1 (or simply "3") automatically meant a fast tempo, while 3/2 was a slow tempo. With the advent of tempo designations such as "adagio" and "allegro," the meaning of meter signatures began to change. What is seen in Castello's music is ample documentation for the growing independence of tempo and meter. His tempo designations appear to have an emotional as much as a mathematical meaning, in keeping with Monteverdian precepts. Allegro meant "cheerful" as much as it did "fast," while adagio indicated "contemplative" as much as "slow." The meaning of the designation *affetto*, used sporadically in Venice throughout the seventeenth century, is uncertain; in Castello's time it seems to have been reserved for quasi-homophonic passages in a slow tempo. In fact, tempo rubato is appropriate for some of the rhapsodic solos in these sonatas.

Castello's vocabulary includes several refinements of "slow," "fast," "loud," and "soft"—among them *Più adagio* (slower), *Adagio adagio* (very slow), and *pianin* (very soft). Dynamics and tempo markings were undoubtedly useful to performers, but except in such works as Monteverdi's *Tancredi* they were rarely to be seen again in Venice until the time of Vivaldi.

For the time these works were written, Castello used an exceptional number of slurs. Since slurs occur in string and wind parts but not in keyboard parts, they probably designated single bows or breaths. The slurs in 1658b, an Antwerp edition, usually cover only two notes, seemingly as a result of mechanical limitations in the printing process.

Ornamentation

Castello's sonatas contain more written ornaments and divisions than the works of most of his contemporaries. Yet even Castello used melodic formulas to imply certain routine embellishments. Divisions are a conspicuous feature of the allegro movements, the object being to replace in performance the long notes of written scores with decorative motives in shorter note values. A Castello passage such as

can be understood to be a decorated version of:

Whenever the same note pattern is applied to a series of notes, sequences result. A rare case in which a melodic figure of this kind seems to be represented by an abbreviation occurs in Sonata 9 of Book I (Part I, p. 40, mm. 21-22, bsn.), where we find the passage:

The context suggests that what was actually intended was:

Except in those marked *affetto*, the majority of Castello's slow movements (being homophonic) do not require the elaborate embellishment associated with the slow movements of a century later. However, some improvisation is acceptable in these movements. According to the advice of Giovanni Bassano in his treatise of 1592 (*Motetti, madrigali et canzoni francese . . . diminuiti per sonar*), divisions should be added to only one part at a time. Bassano sanctioned the elimination of the remaining ensemble parts; accordingly a canzona à 4 could, through the elaboration of the treble part and the elimination of alto, tenor, and bass parts, be converted into a solo sonata. However, it seems unlikely that Castello intended his homophonic movements to be performed very differently from the way they were written. Solo sonatas were written as solo sonatas by Castello's time, and Castello himself was always careful to designate solo parts (note the explicit detail given in the solos in the sonatas of Books I and II).

A discussion of specific types of ornaments found in Castello's sonatas follows.

PASSING ORNAMENTS

By the last quarter of the sixteenth century there was a clear separation of incidental or passing ornamentation and terminal ornamentation. This functional difference was recognized by the terms *passaggi* and *cadentie* in Bassano's treatise of 1586 (*Ricercate, passaggi, et cadentie*). The most common passing ornament used by Castello is signified by the sign *t*, which appears to have multiple meanings. Most commonly it occurs on a dotted eighth-note descending to a sixteenth:

In such a context *t* may have been an abbreviation for *trillo*, but this does not altogether settle the matter of how it was executed. In Giulio Caccini's famous treatise *Le nuove musiche* (1602) the *trillo* was described as an ornament limited to one pitch but executed in progressively shorter note values. The modern trill with an afterbeat, which can easily be accommodated in passages such as that above, e.g.:

could still be designated at this time by the term *groppo*.[10] However, the Italian *groppo* as well as the English "trill" were both associated with cadences. Since Castello also used the sign *t* to indicate cadential ornaments, it seems that he used the sign generically for all ornaments rather than exclusively for the *trillo* or the *groppo*. Since the *t* sign so often occurs in the context of short notes in a fast tempo, it is conceivable that all that was intended was a short ornament of the mordent or inverted mordent type that amounted to no more than a division. A possible execution using the inverted mordent (*tremoletto*) would be:

The insertion of short trills in descending scales had become so common by the eighteenth century that in a 1715 edition of Corelli's solo sonatas Opus 5 (first published in 1700) the even notation

was understood to indicate:

(Note the superficial similarity in this transformation to *notes inégales*.) In fact, this understanding may already have existed in Castello's day, for the *t* is occasionally used in passages of even eighths like that shown above.

Another embellishment in fashion in the 1620s was the *tremolo,* a rapid, steady reiteration of a single pitch, occasionally played with an afterbeat. In most cases all the notes were written out and the designation *tremolo* appeared as well. The indication in the cornett parts of Sonata 17 of Book II (Part II, p. 98, mm. 19-20)

probably refers to an ornament in this general category. The four-note ornament

may be a shorthand indication for the eight-note figure of Sonata 17.[11] Out of context, it looks like a reasonable abbreviation for a modern trill, but underlying harmony or surrounding melody sometimes rules this out as a possibility. *Tremolo* scoring was cultivated in Venice in conjunction with the *stile concitato.* Instances of *tremolo* in instrumental works were produced by Marini (1617/8), Francesco and Gabriel Usper (1619), and Riccio (1621).

There is very little evidence for the use of *notes inégales* in Venice at this time. Occasionally, as in Sonata 17, Book II, a continuo line coincides better with the ensemble if eighths are dotted or dotted notes double-dotted. But only accompanists seem to have been affected by the use of *notes inégales.* The extent to which they were affected depends, at times, on which interpretation of Castello's *t* was followed.

Cadential Ornaments

Castello rarely bothers to indicate cadential ornaments. The modern trill (*groppo*) was commonly suggested by the rhythm ♩ ♩ ♩ | 𝅝 |. Marini shows a simple, even execution in his Opus 8

while other sources of the period, including Bernhard Schmid's tablature version (1607) of some Gabrieli organ works, suggest a more florid rendering:

The *groppo* is implied in Castello's works chiefly in overlapping and sectional, rather than final, closes. Occasionally there appears a *t* sign preceded by a falling figure which itself required elaboration. A Castello *groppo* written thus:

should probably be played approximately in this manner:

(An extra subdivision of the last beat is shown consistently in the 1629 edition of Book I.) Castello's final cadences frequently consist of two parts—a so-called lombard rhythm (♪♩·) and a written trill with afterbeat, e.g.:

It is possible that the lombard rhythm may have been an abbreviation for a backfall

as it was in English sources of the same century.

Freer ornamentation in the manner of a cadenza was sometimes used. There is a written cadenza for the bassoon at the end of the first movement of Sonata 9 of Book I. It is more difficult to say where a cadenza might have been improvised in the sonatas, but the abrupt ending of Sonata 7 of Book II seems to be an appropriate place:

Editorial Procedures

All titles, subtitles, and directives (such as "full accompaniment" and "echo") are translated from the original Italian. Instrumental designations have been translated from the Italian as follows: *violino* = violin; *violetta* = viola or tenor violin (depending on range); *viola* = cello; *cornetto* = cornett; *trombone* = tenor or bass trombone (depending on range); *fagotto* = bassoon. Designations in brackets replace the general designation *Sopran* (=any treble instrument). The barring in this edition follows modern practice, coinciding largely with the composer's indications except insofar as Castello often omits the bar before the final note of a cadence in the upper parts and miscellaneously in the continuo.

Movements in duple meter and slow sections in triple meter are unreduced; fast sections in triple meter are reduced by half. It should be noted, however, that the sign C is replaced in both Antwerp editions—1656e and 1658b—by the sign ¢ (the barring is unchanged). Light double bars, which are editorial, signal rapid or abrupt changes in tempo. The original meter designations, where altered, are indicated in the Critical Notes. Tempo markings are original unless placed in brackets.

Tempo changes are more numerous than meter changes in Castello's works. It seems somewhat artificial to speak of "movements" in the sonatas since pauses (suggested by fermatas) do not coincide necessarily with changes in meter or tempo. At the least, Castello intended no pause before the start of a solo; he is careful to change meters one measure earlier than is customary in modern practice, forcing an entry into the new movement in order to complete the cadence of the last. Although modern practice in barring has been followed, Castello's intention is respected by the indication [attacca].

Superscript brackets (⌐ ¬) indicate the presence of black notation (e.g., ● ▬) in the source. Castello used this reverse color notation to call attention to syncopation. Curiously, no black notation occurs in Book I.

The thirty-second-rest was apparently unknown in Venice in Castello's time. Wherever such a rest appears in this edition, a sixteenth-rest is present in the source. The original rhythm of each passage converted here to *notes inégales* is given in a footnote.

All indications of slurs, ornaments, and dynamics are original unless shown in brackets. There are, of course, some discrepancies among editions. The most glaring are cited in the Critical Notes; to list all would have been meaningless, since only one edition—1658a—differs seriously from the others: it shows much less refinement in notating slurs, ornaments, and dynamics.

Castello's *t* has been left unaltered where it is a passing ornament and seems to demand something other than a trill. The placement of possible cadential trills is indicated by the editorial sign [*tr*], and Castello's *t* has been modified to *t*[*r*] in cadences in which a trill is appropriate.

In Castello's time an accidental sign referred only to the note following it. The present edition conforms to modern practice in that an accidental in the staff applies throughout the measure. Notes lacking accidentals in the source are provided with superscript indications here. Redundant accidentals and meaningless discrepancies between editions have been eliminated. Discrepancies with less certain resolutions are cited in the Critical Notes. Cautionary accidentals introduced by the editor are given in parentheses.

Some of Castello's harmonic usage may seem unusually pungent for the time. There are frequent situations in which either cross-relations in the harmony or an augmented second in a melodic line must be used. Examination of music by Castello's contemporaries shows that both were permissible. Similarly, tritones were used more freely than in Renaissance vocal music. There are numerous afterbeating fifths and octaves, even between outer parts.

As for the more universal problem of *musica ficta*, or unwritten accidentals, one sees Castello very much caught up in the transition from the contrapuntal emphasis of the sixteenth century to the harmonic emphasis of the later seventeenth. In instrumental music of the kind Castello wrote, rhythmic regularity is a far more important factor than in the vocal polyphony of his predecessors. This inevitably brings a stronger harmonic orientation. It would appear that in most cases the mode is controlled by the pulse, with alterations being introduced principally at the bar-line. Cadences, with their own well-worn conventions, are often an exception. Indeed, all views of *musica ficta* in Venetian music of this time are speculative, and the performer is at liberty to make any changes he deems appropriate.

Instruments named in brackets are editorial suggestions, but specific options not in brackets (e.g., trombone or cello) originate with Castello. Most parts are given in modern treble and bass clefs in the transcriptions. The alto clef is retained in parts for the viola. The tenor clef is retained in some of the higher-pitched passages for trombone. Where the clef has been changed in the transcriptions, the original clef is shown in cue-size notation.

Figuration was used sparingly in Venetian works of this time, and no effort has been made to figure every note of the basso continuo. Figures in brackets are editorial insertions introduced only when the realization given cannot be inferred from the ensemble parts or from Castello's own figures. Castello's "6" may refer to either a first or a second inversion. His two-part harmony often leaves a specific triadic identity undetermined.

Dynamics markings *per se* are absent from Castello's basso continuo, although the term *eco* usually occurs in conjunction with a *p* in the ensemble parts. There are numerous instructions concerning instrumentation, texture, and so forth; any of these that have been deleted are cited in the Critical Notes.

The most efficient way of indicating the various peculiarities of the two-stave continuo part to Sonata 17 of Book II has been to reproduce it together with a traditional realization. The purpose of the upper staff was to give the accompanist some idea of the intricacies in the ensemble parts. Such two-stave continuos were used in numerous violin sonatas of the time, including Castello's own Sonatas 1 and 2 of Book II and the solo sonatas in Marini's Opus 8 and Fontana's volume of sonatas. However, it is not inconceivable that this two-stave arrangement was sometimes used as the skeleton for a keyboard sonata; here there was a precedent in the keyboard partitura (1601) of Gioseffo Guami's ensemble *Canzonette* (1612). Castello's score can also be usefully compared with the unusual sonata for organ and optional trombone in Marini's Opus 8.

Critical Notes

These notes refer to discrepancies between the present edition and the seventeenth-century editions of Books I and II. Comments refer to all extant editions or parts if not qualified. Parts are designated by species (e.g., Canto I) if the instrumentation is variable or unspecified. In cases of specific instrumentation, the following abbreviations are used: vn. = violin; cor. = cornett; bsn. = bassoon; tbn. = trombone; vla. = viola; b.c. = basso continuo. The usual system of pitch designation—wherein middle c is c', two-line c is c'', and so forth—is used.

Book I, Sonata 3

P. 4, original meter and rhythm of the Allegro are 3, dotted half, two eighths, half. P. 5, m. 18, change to duple meter occurs here. P. 5 ff., mm. 2, 4, 14, 16, no slurs in 1658a. P. 8, m. 28, b.c., beat 4, sharp sign is beside the note-head. P. 9, m. 6, Canto I, dynamic marking is *p* in 1629e and 1658a, and omitted in 1658b. P. 10, m. 11, b.c., beat 4, bass figure retains the sharp. M. 14, Canto I, final note is sharp.

Book I, Sonata 5

P. 12, the second instrument is designated as *"trombon overo violetta."* P. 15, m. 36, Canto I, beats 3-4, rhythm, sixteenth, dotted eighth, sixteenth, dotted eighth; tbn., note 6 is a' in 1658a. P. 16, the original meter and rhythm are $\frac{3}{2}$, dotted half, quarter, dotted half, quarter, dotted half, quarter, except in Canto I of 1658b where the meter is $\frac{3}{1}$. P. 16, m. 5, Canto I, note 2 is b'; tbn. and b.c., note 2 is f; tbn., note 3 is e in 1658b. An f in the bass would be harmonically acceptable but would not adhere to the melodic pattern present. P. 16, m. 6, tbn., note 1 is d in 1658a, note 2 is c in 1629e and 1658a. P. 16, m. 14, change to duple meter occurs here. P. 18, m. 11, Canto I, beat 4, ornament here consisting of last 4 notes written as sixteenths in 1658a. P. 19, m. 22, tbn., notation would seem to suggest that a cadenza should be inserted here. P. 20, the original meter of Presto is 3, quarter, quarter, quarter.

Book I, Sonata 9

P. 26, mm. 11-beat 1 of m. 12, b.c., all notes are a third lower. P. 27, m. 15, b.c., notes 2-3 are B-E in 1658a. P. 28, m. 24, vn. I, beat 4, ornament consists of the last 4 notes written as sixteenths in 1658a. P. 29, meter is 3, dotted half, quarter, half; were it not for the fact that the "Adagio" indication appears in all three editions, one would expect this section to be performed as an Allegro. P. 30, mm. 15-16, b.c., this part is written a third higher in 1658a. P. 31, m. 25, bsn., final note is not flatted in 1658a. P. 32, m. 2, vn. II, note 1 is e''. P. 33, m. 11, vn. I, note 8 is g'' in 1629e and 1658a. P. 34, m. 15, vn. I, tempo marking absent. M. 16, vn. I, beat 4, ornament consists of last four notes written as sixteenths in 1658a. P. 35, m. 22, b.c., notes 3-4, 8ve higher in 1629e, notes 2-4, 9th higher in 1658a. M. 30, bsn., notes 2-3 are thirty-seconds. M. 31, bsn., note 7 is A. P. 36, original meter and rhythm of the Allegro are 3, dotted half, quarter, half. All slurs in the vn. parts are present in all editions except 1658a. M. 9, vn. I, dynamic marking is *p* in 1658a and 1658b. P. 39, m. 16, vn. I, beat 4, ornament consists of last four notes written as sixteenths in 1658a. P. 39 ff., mm. 18-21, vn. II, *pianin* is the dynamic marking. P. 40, mm. 19-20, b.c., tied note is B in 1629e. M. 21, bsn., beats 3-4 written eighth (E), dotted eighth (F), sixteenth (G) in 1629e and 1658b. M. 22, bsn., beats 1-2 written eighth (C), eighth (E), dotted eighth (F), sixteenth (G) in 1629e and 1658b. Divisions are included in the bsn. part in mm. 21-22 in the present edition because they seem to be required for consistency. M. 21 (beats 3-4) and m. 22 (beats 1-2), bsn., these notes are a third higher in 1658a than in the other two editions. P. 41, mm. 25-29, all parts, alternate *t* signs are present in all editions except 1658a.

Book I, Sonata 12

Third part is designated for *"trombon overo violetta."* P. 42, mm. 2-29 *passim*, the modal contradiction in the theme must have been intended, for nowhere is there any accidental or figure to suggest the use of C-sharps (or other analogous tones). M. 3, beat 4, b.c., the figure $\frac{\#6}{\#3}$ would derive from a literal reading of the ensemble parts, but if it is used in the realization it would produce uncharacteristic progressions and myriad violations of the rules of part-leading. The conflicting elements that occur in any solution to this continuo derive ultimately from the conceptual inconsistency in Castello's time between a horizontally maintained ensemble and a vertically maintained accompaniment. P. 46, m. 6, vn. I, rhythm, whole-note in 1658a. P. 50, the original instruction in the b.c. is *"Si sona solo il Basso principale sino alla tripola"* ("Only the principal accompaniment instrument [i.e., the keyboard] plays until the triple-meter sign"). P. 52, the original meter sign of the Allegro is 3, half, half, half. M. 3, b.c., sharp under beat 3 deleted. M. 8, vn. I, beat 2 has a *t* sign in 1658a. Pp. 52-54, mm. 8-33, all parts, alternate *t* signs present in all editions except 1658a. P. 53, m. 13, b.c., figure 6 occurs here. P. 55, m. 40, tbn., meter change occurs here in 1658a. P. 56, mm. 7-14, m. 16, slurs in vn. parts present in all editions except 1658a. P. 61, m. 21, b.c., beat 3, figure "6" occurs here. P. 62, m. 33, vn. I, beat 4, *t* sign here in 1658a; original rhythmic notation in this m. is ♪ ♪ ♪ ♪ ♪ ♪, etc. P. 63, m. 40, b.c., two superfluous beats occur here in 1658a.

Book II, Sonata 7

P. 3, m. 23, Canto I, notes 3-4 are b'-a' in 1629f and 1644e. P. 6, the original meter and rhythm of the Allegro are 3, half, half, half. M. 4, bsn., note 3 is flatted; flat is canceled in this edition by analogy with Canto I, m. 9. P. 8, mm. 23-24, accent marks omitted; they are added in the present edition to indicate syncopation. M. 35, change to duple meter occurs here. P. 10, m. 12, Canto I, note 4 is g'-sharp. M. 23, bsn., note 12 is not flatted in 1629f. P. 11, m. 26, bsn., notes 1-3 are sixteenth, thirty-second, thirty-second.

Book II, Sonata 11

P. 14, m. 1, the third instrument was designated as *"trombon overo viola."* P. 15, m. 14 and m. 15, b.c., beat 1 of each measure has a sharp figuration in bass. P. 18, the original meter and rhythm of the Presto are 3, quarter, quarter, quarter, quarter, quarter, quarter. P. 23, m. 39, tbn., superfluous whole-rest in 1644e. P. 25, m. 52, Canto II, note 2 preceded by a natural sign. Pp. 25-26, mm. 3-4, tbn., rests omitted in these measures in 1644e. P. 27, m. 11, original tempo indication is *"Adagio adagio."*

Book II, Sonata 12

P. 28, m. 1, the third instrument was designated as *"trombon overo viola"* (*"overo violetta"* appears in some partbooks). P. 34, m. 7, Canto I, tempo indication omitted in 1644e. M. 9, b.c., sharp moved from figured bass to note 2 in 1644e. M. 11, b.c., note 3 is e in 1644e. M. 15, tbn., note 2 is g in 1644e. P. 35, m. 1, the original meter and rhythm of the Allegro are 3, dotted half, quarter, quarter, quarter. P. 39, m. 38, change to duple meter occurs here. P. 40, mm. 8-9, tbn., sextuplets are notated as thirty-seconds; they are grouped by sixes and barred by twelves, although the figure "6" does not appear. P. 41, mm. 11-16, all parts, accent marks do not appear in the original. M. 16, Canto II, note 1 is a'-sharp. P. 42, Canto II, note 4 is sharp. P. 43, mm. 12-13, Cantos I and II, sextuplets are notated as described in entry for p. 40, mm. 8-9. M. 14, Canto I, beat 2, rhythm is thirty-second, dotted sixteenth; several other resolutions for this measure are possible. M. 14, Canto II, beats 2-3, rhythm is thirty-second, dotted sixteenth, thirty-second, dotted sixteenth, sixteenth, dotted eighth. P. 44, mm. 15-20, all parts, accent marks do not appear in the original. P. 45, m. 26, Canto I, note 8 is e'' in 1644e. P. 46, m. 30, tbn., note 1 is g in 1644e. P. 49, mm. 52-53, Canto II, final note of m. 52 and all notes of m. 53 are a second lower in 1644e.

Book II, Sonata 15

P. 50, m. 1, original designations of the instruments are *"violino," "violetta," "violetta,"* and *"viola."* M. 3, vn. II, note 2 is g' in 1629f. P. 51, m. 1, b.c., there is an indication "Fuga sola" here and at the beginnings of the Allegros on pages 53, 57, and 60. It means "Do not harmonize the first entry of the subject," a command inspired by the fifth rule for realizing a basso continuo given by Lodovico Viadana in the preface to his *Cento concerti ecclesiastici* (1602). P. 55, m. 17, vn. II, note 3 is g' in 1644e. M. 19, the original meter and rhythm for the Adagio are 3, half, half, half. P. 56, m. 33, vla., note 2 is g', producing parallel fifths with vn. II.

Book II, Sonata 16

P. 60, m. 1, original designations of the instruments are *"violino," "violetta," "violetta,"* and *"viola."* The original meter and rhythm of the Allegro are C 3, half, quarter, quarter, quarter, quarter in 1629f and 1644e, and 3, half, quarter, quarter, quarter, quarter in 1656e. P. 65, m. 33, vla. I, note 1 is f'. P. 67, m. 54, b.c., natural of figured bass appears before note 1 (d''). P. 69, m. 81, vn. I, notes 3 and 4 are e' and f'. P. 72, m. 30, vla. II, dynamics marked *p* here in 1644e. P. 73, m. 32, vla. II, beat 1, rhythm, eighth, sixteenth, sixteenth. M. 32, cello, one sixteenth-note omitted in 1644e; in 1656e beat 1 rhythm is eighth, sixteenth, sixteenth. P. 74, m. 1, original meter and rhythm of the Allegro are 3, half, half, quarter, quarter. P. 76, m. 31, vn. I, rhythm is whole-note, half-rest in 1644e. M. 31, cello, rest is omitted in 1644e and 1656e, and there is a superfluous rest in this measure in 1629f. M. 39, vn. I, rhythm is whole-note, half-rest in 1644e.

Book II, Sonata 17

P. 81, the first basso continuo is a *partitura* given in the source. It is shown here in its entirety for the purpose of reference rather than performance; accordingly, all the original instructions are retained. The second basso continuo is a modern realization for use in performance. The replying instruments should be offstage (this arrangement was specified in an echo sonata for three violins in Marini's Opus 8). If this arrangement is adopted, a second double bass (or similar instrument) should be used to accompany these instruments. If no double bass is used and the echoing instruments are placed at a distance, the keyboard continuo should cease. If the echoing instruments remain within the ensemble, and no double bass is used, the bass notes may be taken by the keyboard. P. 88, mm. 3-4, vn. and upper staff of b.c., beats 3 and 4 of both measures, rhythm, ♪ 𝅘𝅥𝅰𝅘𝅥𝅰𝅘𝅥𝅰 𝅘𝅥𝅰𝅘𝅥𝅰𝅘𝅥𝅰 𝅘𝅥𝅰𝅘𝅥𝅰𝅘𝅥𝅰 . M. 5, vn. and upper staff of b.c., rhythm, 𝅘𝅥𝅰𝅘𝅥𝅰𝅘𝅥𝅰 𝅘𝅥𝅰𝅘𝅥𝅰𝅘𝅥𝅰 𝅘𝅥𝅰𝅘𝅥𝅰𝅘𝅥𝅰 𝅘𝅥𝅰𝅘𝅥𝅰𝅘𝅥𝅰 . P. 90, m. 13, b.c., if "basso" means an instrument of bass register reinforcing the lower staff, then the only accompaniment here should be by that instrument; if one takes "basso" to mean "basso principale" (as literally given in Sonata 12 of Book I) and the replying instruments are separated from the principal ensemble instruments in performance, then the echo effects will be contradicted by the keyboard's sounding from a different direction, an unlikely intention. The notes occurring on the upper staff of the original b.c. in mm. 13-20 were ostensibly intended as cues. P. 91, m. 17, beats 3-4, vn., rhythm, eighth-rest, 8 thirty-second-notes. In 1629f the eighth-rest has been emended by hand to be a quarter-rest. The resolution given in the present edition is modeled on pp. 96-97, mm. 11-12, but other interpretations are possible. M. 18, replying vn., beat 2, the four sixteenths are four thirty-seconds. P. 95, mm. 4-5, b.c. of original continuo, beat 4 of each measure is eighth-note, eighth-note. P. 96, m. 10, b.c., see entry for p. 90, m. 13, b.c. P. 99, m. 5, vn., notes 5-8 are f'', a'', g'', f''. P. 100, m. 8, replying instruments, the notation *"insieme"* (together) has been deleted here and in m. 20, and also from the principal parts at m. 19; "solo" cues have been deleted at mm. 12 and 14. M. 8, b.c., see entry for p. 90, m. 13, b.c. P. 101, m. 26, cor. and vn., the presence of fermatas here suggests that the final echo was to be retarded.

Acknowledgments

Grateful acknowledgment is made to the Trustees of the Bodleian Library for permission to reproduce the two photographs of Castello's music; also to the staffs of the Bodleian, the Library of the Dean and Chapter, Durham Cathedral, the British Museum, the Biblioteka Uniwersytecka, Wrocław (formerly Breslau), and the Fondazione Giorgio Cini for their kind assistance in making available the sources used in preparing this edition.

September 1976

Eleanor Selfridge-Field
Mills College

Notes

[1] Eleanor Selfridge-Field, "Dario Castello: A Non-Existent Biography," *Music and Letters* 53 (1972): 179-90.

[2] Claudio Sartori, *Bibliografia della musica strumentale italiana,* 2 vols. (Florence, 1952-68).

[3] Contrary to the indication in Sartori's *Bibliografia,* I:337.

[4] With slight damage to other parts, contrary to the indication in Sartori, *Bibliografia,* II:95. Also, the reference to *"oboi"* in Sartori's listing for Sonata 17 (*Bibliografia,* II:95) should read *"doi."*

[5] See Eleanor Selfridge-Field, *Venetian Instrumental Music from Gabrieli to Vivaldi* (Oxford and New York), pp. 132-38 *et passim.*

[6] There is a modern edition of this work by Otto Gombosi (Neuilly-sur-Seine, 1955). Capirola's diminutive (see pp. lxvii and 85) was *"pian piano."*

[7] Although the first *violetta* part (i.e., the second part) in Sonatas 15 and 16 of Book II can be played on the violin, the specific use of the term *violetta* indicates that the violin was not really the instrument Castello intended.

[8] Cf. the sonata "La Monica" *à 3* (for two violins and viola da gamba) and the fifth canzona *à 4* (for two violins and two viole da gamba) in Marini's Opus 8 (1626 or 1629).

[9] See the *Canzoni da sonar* (1625) by Giovanni Picchi.

[10] See this usage in Marini's Opus 8.

[11] In either figure the *"t"* could refer only to an afterbeat, since it is usually placed near the end of the slur in the original prints.

Prima Parte.

S O N A T E

C O N C E R T A T E

In ſtil Moderno Per Sonar nel Organo
Ouero Clauicembalo con di‿
uerſi Inſtrumenti.

A 1. 2. 3. & 4. Voci.

DI D. DARIO CASTELLO

Muſico Della Sereniſſima Signoria di Venetia
In S. Marco, & Capo di Compa-
gnia de Inſtrumenti.

LIBRO SECONDO

Nouamente Riſtampato

IN VENETIA MDC XXXXIIII

Appreſſo Bartolomeo Magni.

A

Plate I. Title page from the 1644 edition of Castello's *Sonate concertate*, Book II.
(Courtesy, Bodleian Library)

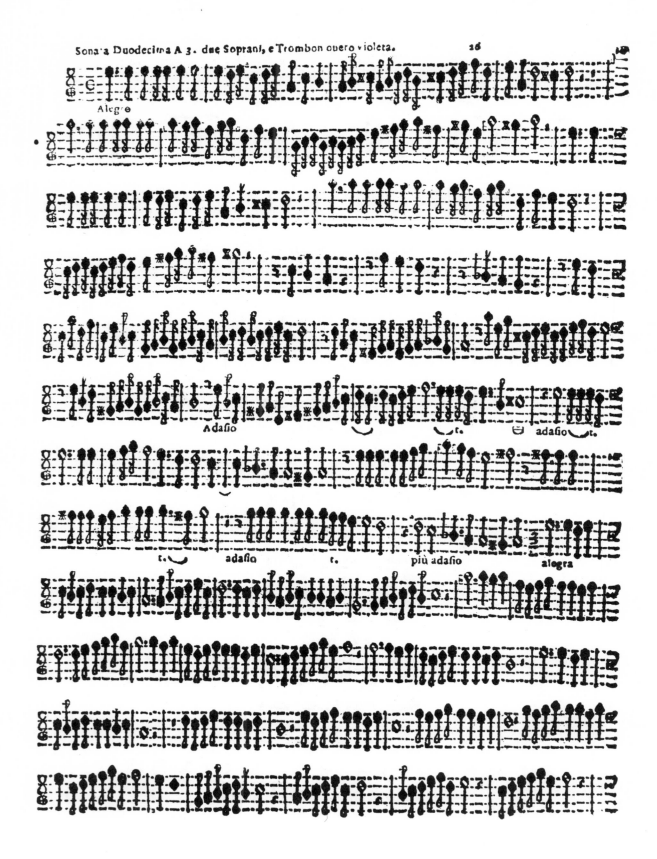

Plate II. Excerpt from a part for unnamed treble instrument in Sonata 12 of
the 1644 edition of Book II. (Courtesy, Bodleian Library)

SELECTED ENSEMBLE SONATAS

Sonatas from *Sonate concertate*, Book I (1621)

Sonata 3
for Two Treble Instruments

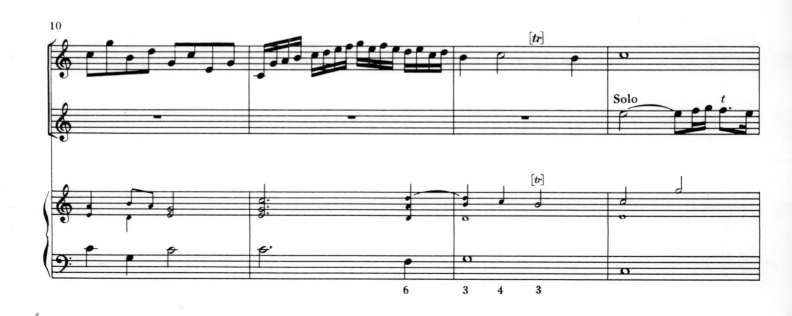

12

Sonata 5
for Treble Instrument and Trombone

13

Adagio

14

Presto 25

30

[Adagio]

[Moderato]

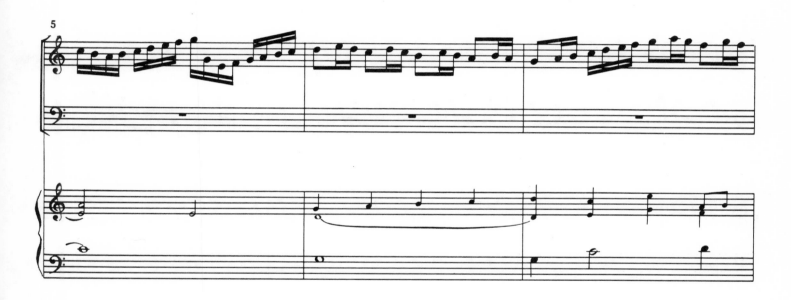

Presto

Sonata 9
for Two Violins and Bassoon

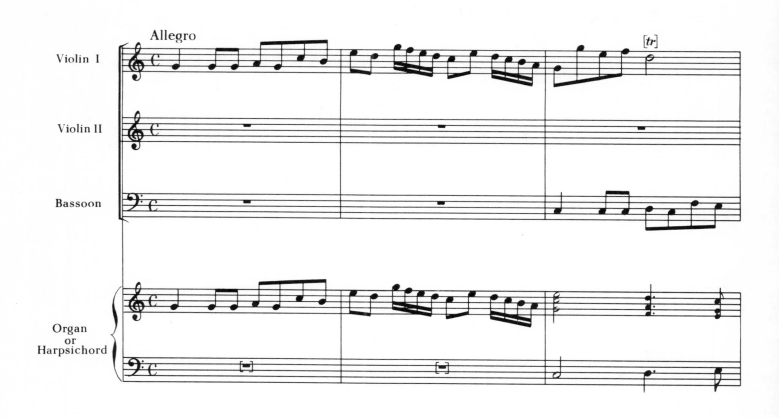

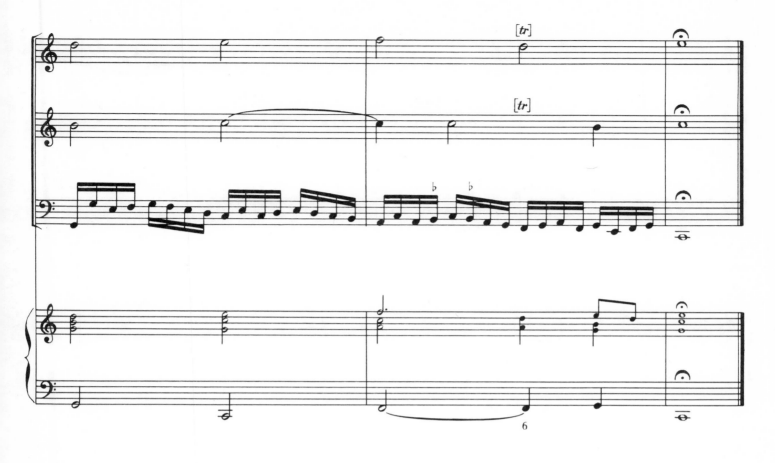

Allegro

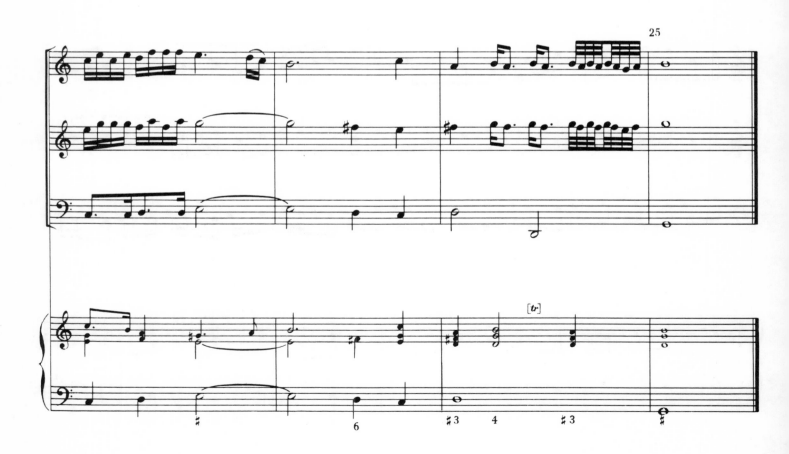

Adagio

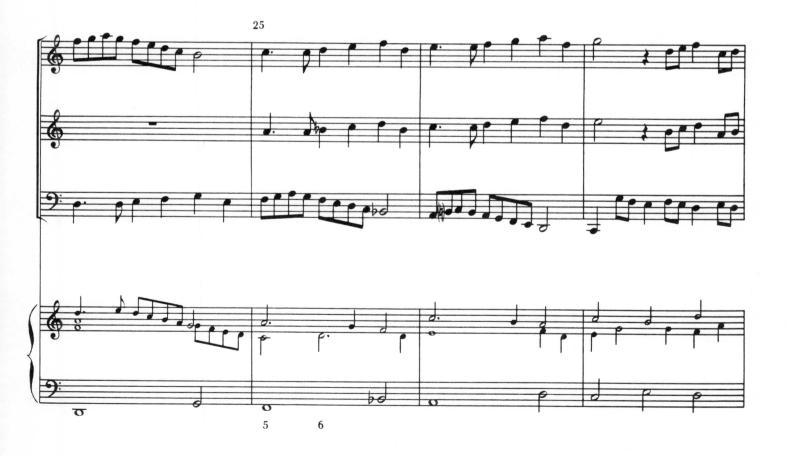

Allegro

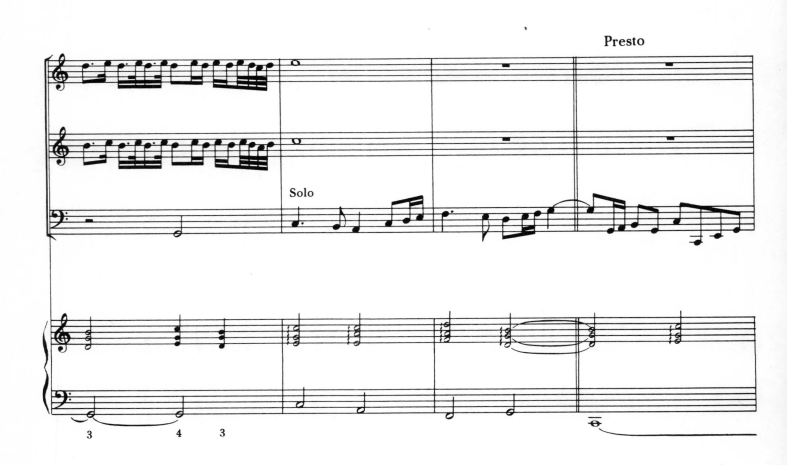

(a) ♩. ♪ ♩. ♪|♩. ♪ in the source

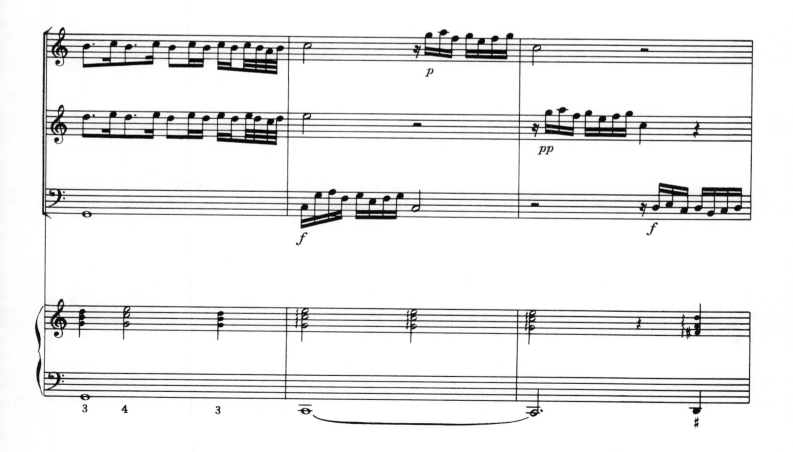

Sonata 12
for Two Violins and Trombone

(a) See the critical commentary for a discussion of this editorial bass figure.

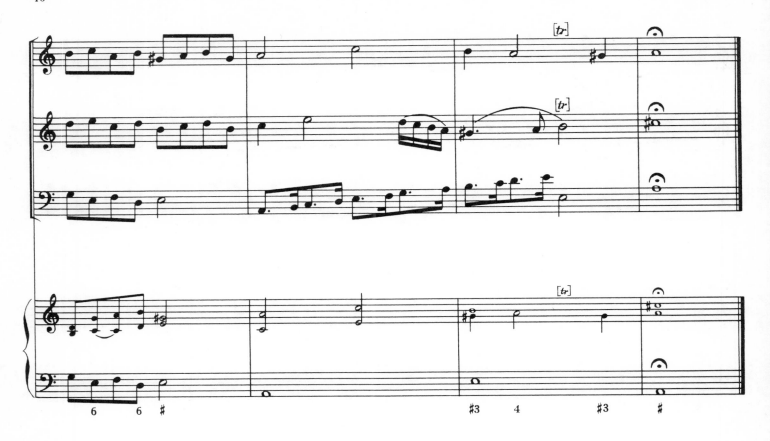

Adagio

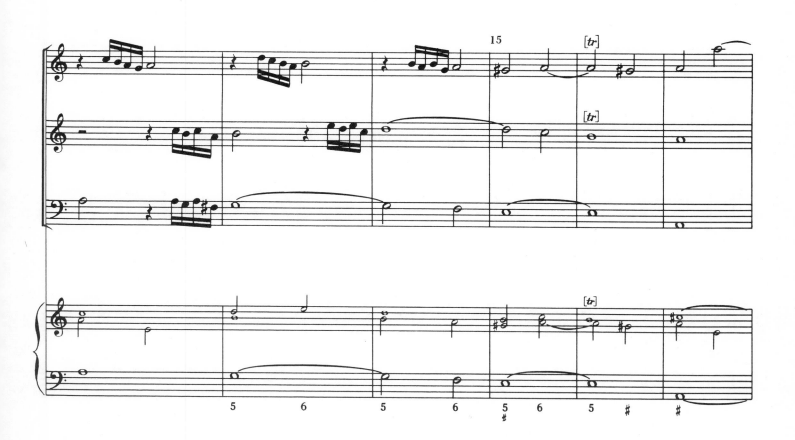

20

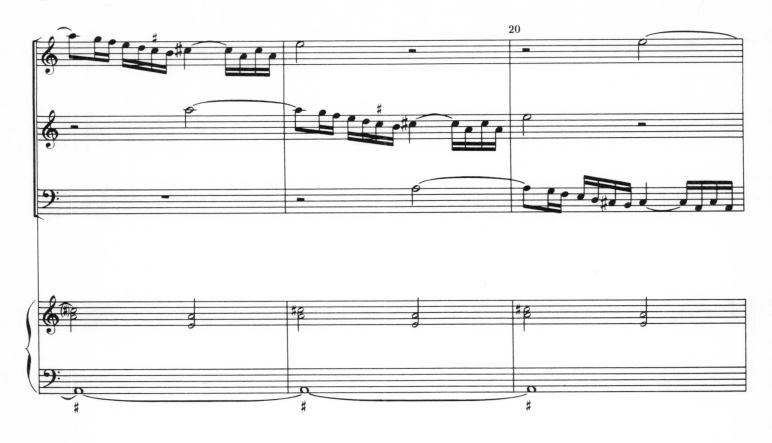

Adagio

Keyboard only

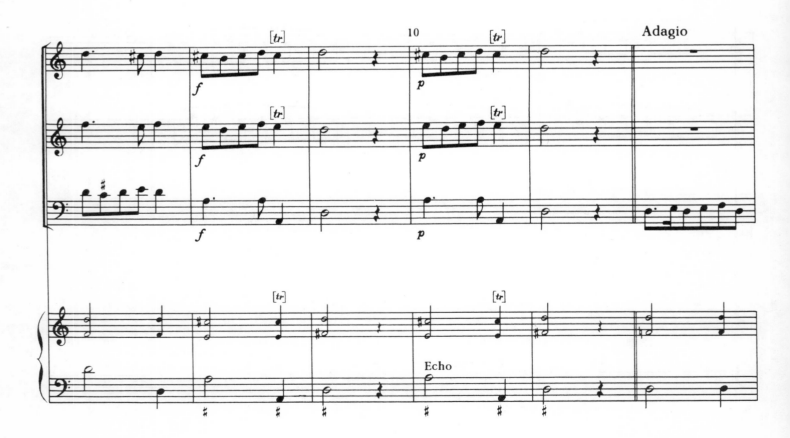

Allegro